Planting a Rainbow

Written and illustrated by
Lois Ehlert

Harcourt Brace & Company

SAN DIEGO   NEW YORK   LONDON

DEDICATED TO SHIRLEY AND DICK

Requests for permission to make copies of any
part of the work should be mailed to:
Permissions Department,
Harcourt Brace & Company, 6277 Sea Harbor Drive,
Orlando, Florida 32887-6777.

Library of Congress Cataloging-in-Publication Data
Ehlert, Lois.
Planting a rainbow.
Summary: A mother and child plant a rainbow of
flowers in the family garden.
ISBN 0-15-262609-3
ISBN 0-15-262610-7 pb
ISBN 0-15-262611-5 oversize pb
[1. Gardening—Fiction.   2. Flowers—Fiction.
3. Mother and child—Fiction.]
I. Title.
PZ7.E3225P1   1988   [E]   87-8528

N M L K J

Printed in Singapore

Planting a Rainbow

Written and illustrated by
Lois Ehlert

Harcourt Brace & Company

SAN DIEGO NEW YORK LONDON

DEDICATED TO SHIRLEY AND DICK

Requests for permission to make copies of any
part of the work should be mailed to:
Permissions Department,
Harcourt Brace & Company, 6277 Sea Harbor Drive,
Orlando, Florida 32887-6777.

Library of Congress Cataloging-in-Publication Data
Ehlert, Lois.
Planting a rainbow.
Summary: A mother and child plant a rainbow of
flowers in the family garden.
ISBN 0-15-262609-3
ISBN 0-15-262610-7 pb
ISBN 0-15-262611-5 oversize pb
[1. Gardening—Fiction.   2. Flowers—Fiction.
3. Mother and child—Fiction.]
I. Title.
PZ7.E3225P1   1988   [E]   87-8528

N M L K J

Printed in Singapore

Every year Mom and
I plant a rainbow.

In the fall we buy some bulbs

orange
tiger lily
bulb

TIGER LILY

red
tulip
bulb

TULIP

orange
tulip
bulb

TULIP

and plant them in the ground.

DAFFODIL

yellow
daffodil
bulb

blue
hyacinth
bulb

HYACINTH

purple
crocus
corm

CROCUS

purple
bearded iris
rhizome

IRIS

We order seeds from catalogs and

Phlox

Morning Glory

Zinnia

wait all winter long

Aster

Cornflower

Marigold

Daisy

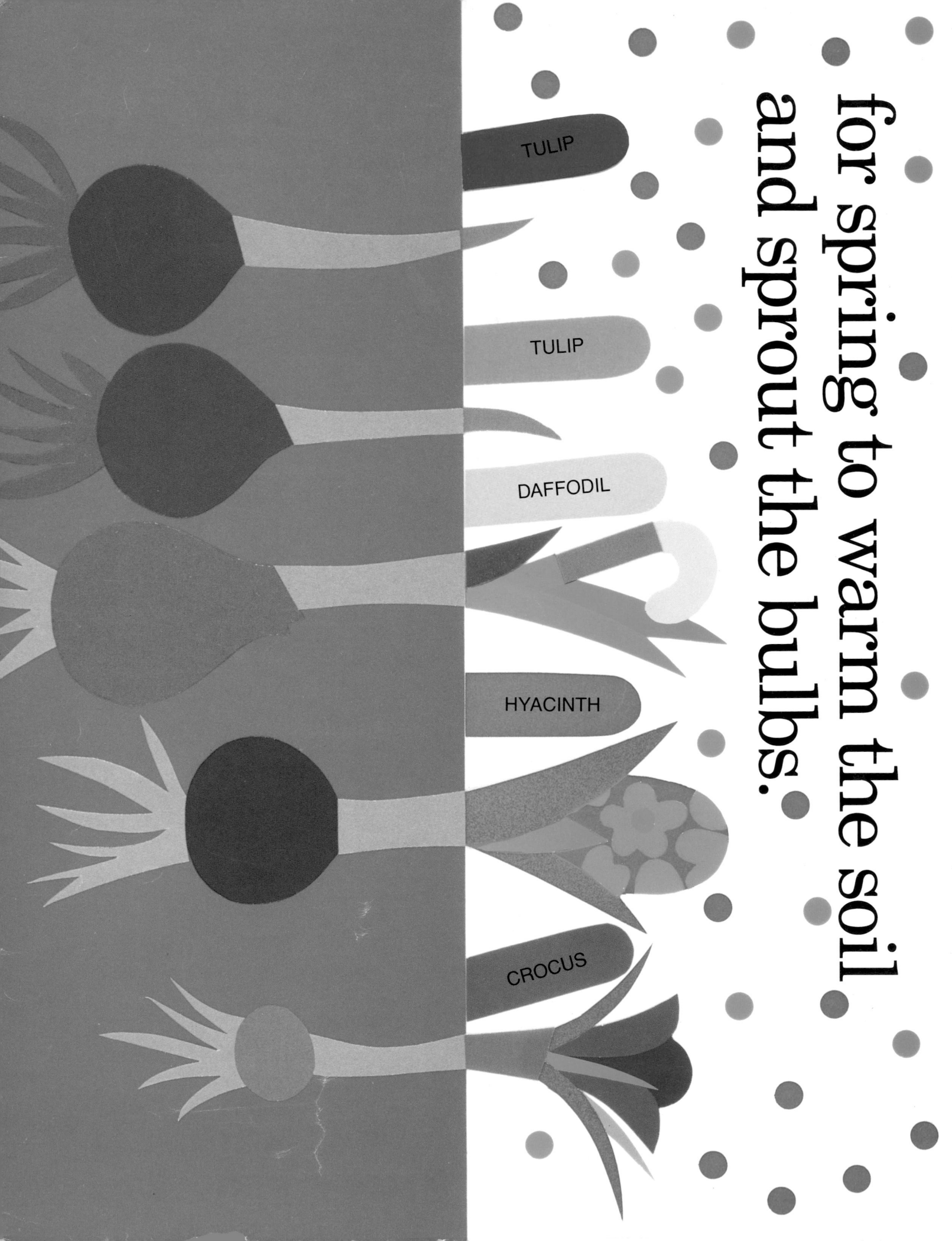

for spring to warm the soil
and sprout the bulbs.

TULIP

TULIP

DAFFODIL

HYACINTH

CROCUS

TULIP

TULIP

DAFFODIL

HYACINTH

CROCUS

Then it's time to go to the garden center to select some seedlings.

DELPHINIUM

POPPY

ROSE

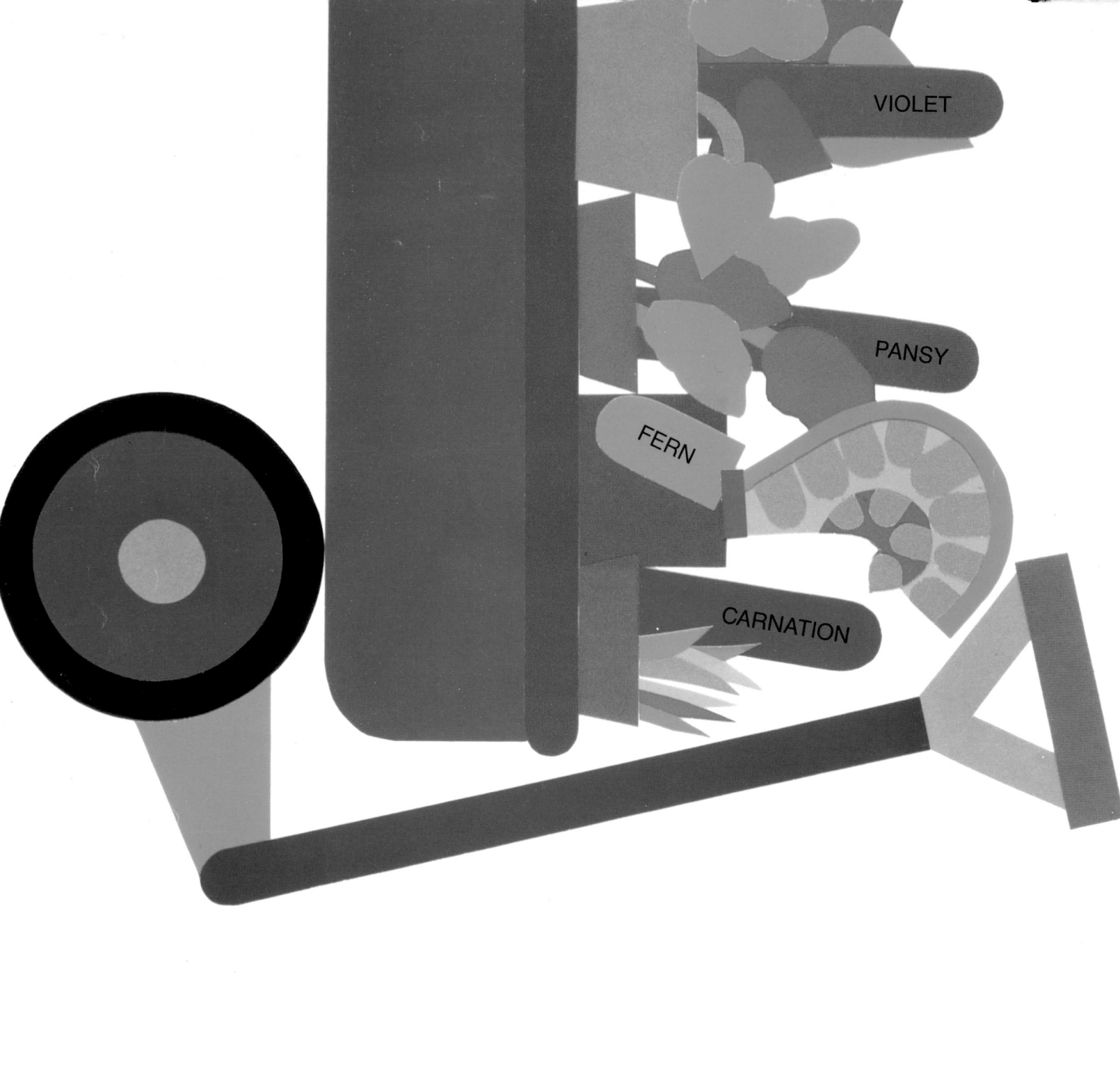

ROSE

TIGER LILY

VIOLET

CARNATION

DAISY

PHLOX

ASTER

DELPHINIUM

We sow the seeds and set out the

plants in soil,

MARIGOLD

POPPY

ZINNIA

PANSY

MORNING GLORY

CORNFLOWER

FERN

IRIS

ROSE

VIOLET

TIGER LILY

CARNATION

DAISY

PHLOX

DELPHINIUM

ASTER

and watch the

rainbow grow,

MARIGOLD

POPPY

ZINNIA

PANSY

MORNING GLORY

CORNFLOWER

FERN

IRIS

and grow,

and grow.

tulips

carnations

poppy

tiger lily

and
some
yellow
blooms.

daisy

marigold

daffodils

We grow something green

ferns

and
some blue
flowers,

morning
glories

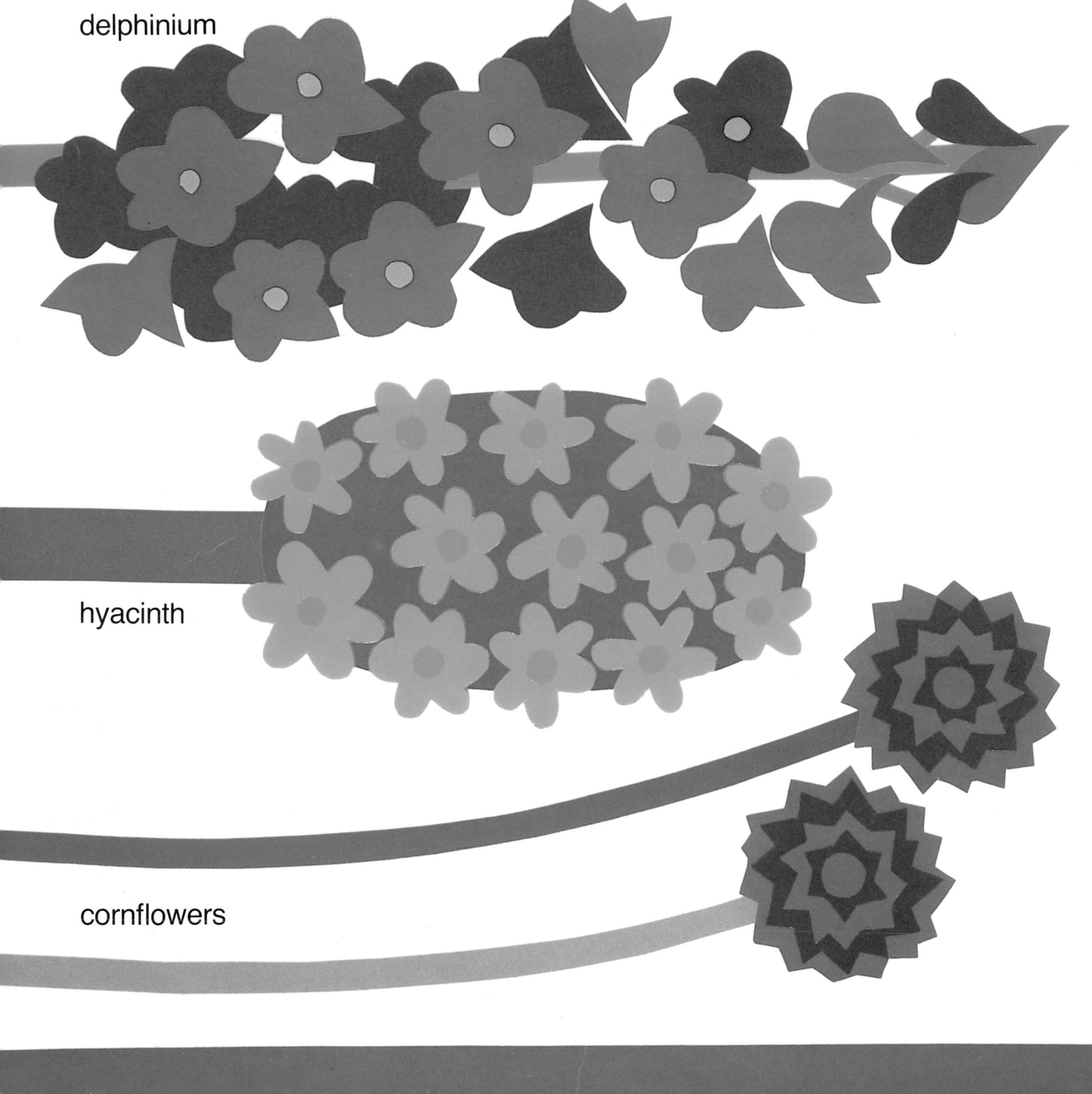

delphinium

hyacinth

cornflowers

and some
purple
flowers,
too.

crocus

phlox

We have
some red
flowers

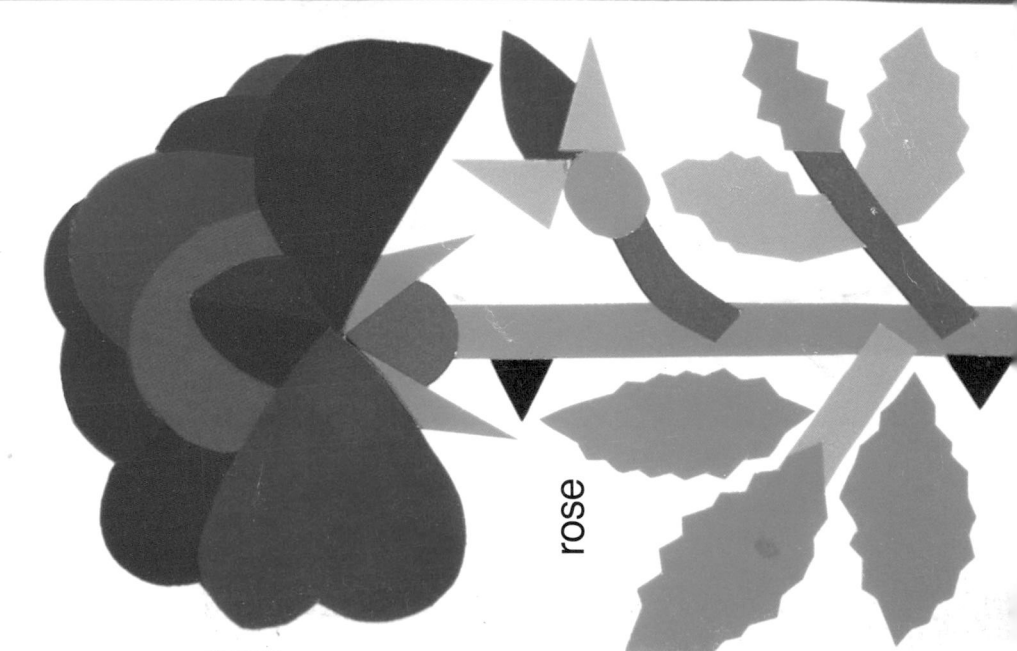

rose

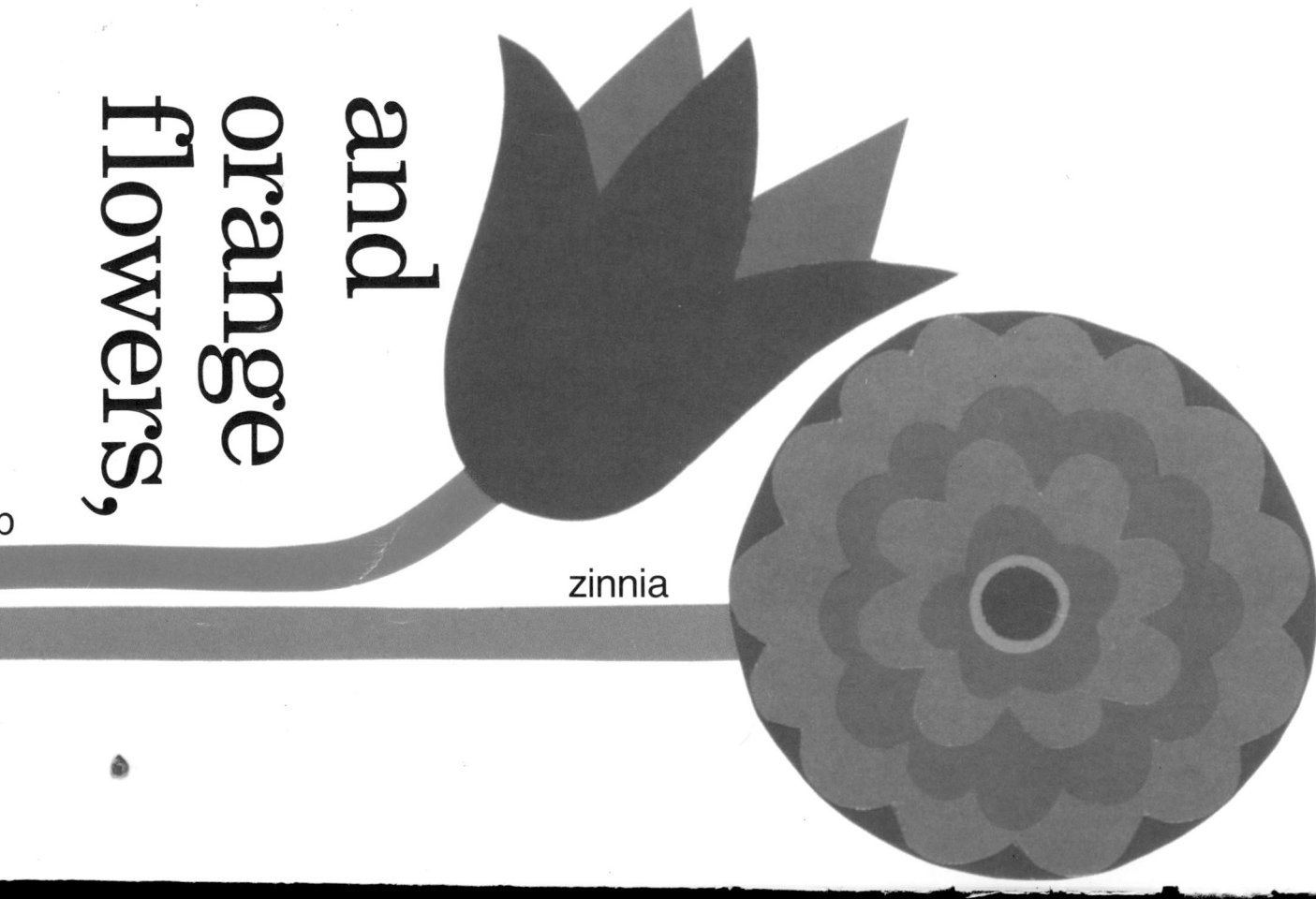

and
orange
flowers,

tulip

zinnia

iris

violets

asters

pansy

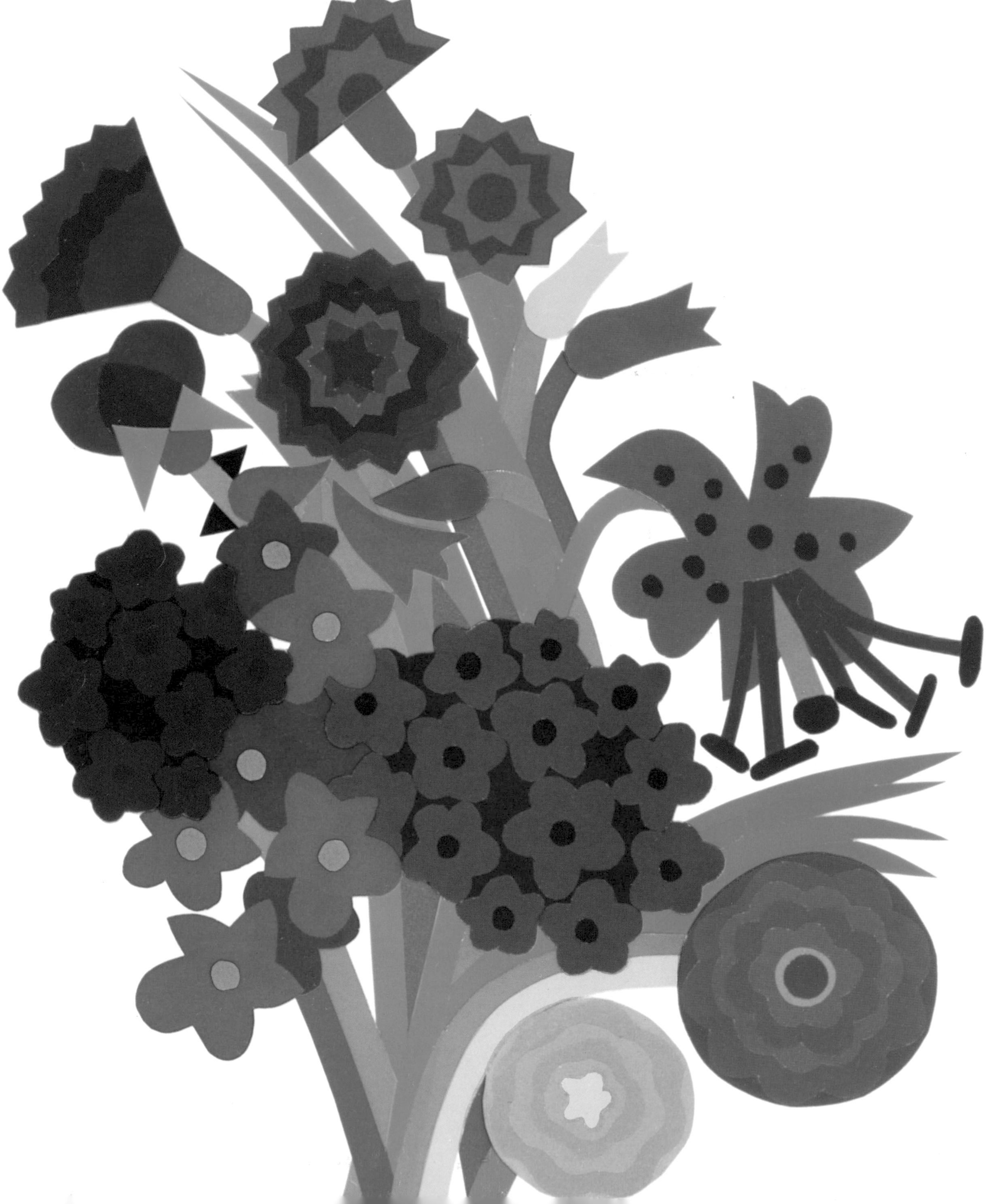

All summer long
we pick them
and bring them home.

And when summer is over, we know we can grow our rainbow again next year.